With thanks to Pia, Mia and Alfie

First published in 2018 in Great Britain by Wildlife Whimsies Publishing
www.wildlifewhimsiespublishing.co.uk

ISBN 978-1-9996246-0-6

Printed in Great Britain

The
DARING DROPLETS
World Water Cycle Team

WRITTEN BY
Tina Talbot

ILLUSTRATED BY
Karina Siba

WILDLIFE WHIMSIES PUBLISHING

Meet the World Water Cycle Team

DRIZZLE is adventurous and sporty. In the winter, he likes ice skating and throwing snowballs at his friends. In the summer, he scuba dives in underground caves and snorkels with sharks. He loves superheroes and secretly wishes he was one.

DRIBBLE enjoys reading stories about mermaids, pirates and the Loch Ness Monster. He also likes spooky ghost stories about haunted lighthouses and exploring the oceans of the world in search of seahorses, shipwrecks and sunken treasure.

DAZZLE sparkles everywhere she goes. She makes the frost glisten on cold winter mornings and dances in the April showers. Her favourite hobbies are swimming with dolphins, splashing in puddles and helping the sun paint rainbows in the sky.

Together, they are known as The Daring Droplets.

One bright sunny day, the Daring Droplets were bobbing in the ocean, ready to start another water cycle and a new adventure.

While they waited, Drizzle announced, "I have an idea! Let's have a race to see which one of us can finish this water cycle first." Dribble and Dazzle both agreed enthusiastically.

The blazing hot sun beamed down and heated the ocean, turning Drizzle, Dribble and Dazzle into mist. "We are evaporating!" cried Drizzle with excitement. The Daring Droplets began their journey, slowly rising into the sky.

As they floated higher and higher, it started to get cold.
"I'm freezing!" complained Dribble.
"Stop moaning!" snapped Drizzle. "It's not freezing, it's just a bit chilly, that's all."
Dazzle looked at her teammates in despair. "Don't squabble you two!" she ordered. "Let's hug each other to keep warm."

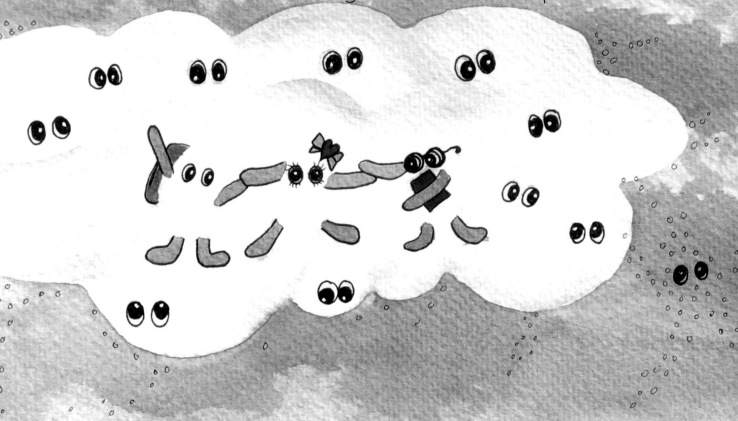

The Daring Droplets were soon joined by other misty droplets who had also evaporated from oceans, rivers and lakes around the world. They all huddled together until, eventually, they turned into a fluffy white cloud.

The cloud grew bigger and heavier as more evaporated droplets joined in. The heavier it became, the darker it got. Finally, it was so dark that Dazzle could not see her teammates anymore. Looking around frantically, she shouted, "Where are you?"

"Over here!" replied Drizzle to her left.

"Over here!" answered Dribble to her right.

Their voices sounded far away. As she searched for them, she realised that their big cloud had broken up into three smaller clouds and the wind was blowing them all in opposite directions!

Drizzle fell out of his cloud first and, to his delight, he had turned into snow. "Geronimo!" he yelled into the cold air. His backpack changed into a parachute and carried him back down to Earth.

Dribble burst out of his cloud as an icy hail stone and immediately got caught in a strong, freezing wind that kept sending him back up into the air. It was like being on a roller coaster ride!

Dazzle dropped out of her cloud as rain and was very pleased to see her pretty pink bow in the reflection of another falling raindrop. "First one back to the ocean is the winner," she thought.

Drizzle landed on a snowy mountain top. "Fantastic!" he exclaimed. "I love skiing!" Whoosh! Whoosh! He zigzagged his way down the mountain, the cold air blowing in his face as he went. He stopped briefly and made a snowman.

Dribble fell into a furiously fast-flowing river. The bracing, bitter cold of the water almost took his breath away. "I'm in a water rapid!" he gasped as he whirled down the choppy channel of water at great speed, holding on to his glasses for dear life.

Dazzle landed in a beautiful green meadow full of pretty flowers and fluttering butterflies. When the sun shone through her, she created a glittering rainbow that cast a magical spell over all the flowers as if they were sprinkled with fairy dust.

Finally, she dropped onto a pink petal and made it sparkle in the sunlight.

Back on the mountainside, the snow had melted and Drizzle turned back into a droplet. He flowed into a river and carried on his journey. "I am going to win the race," he thought competitively.

Then, all of a sudden, everything went dark.
"What's happened?" he asked. "Where am I?"

"I'm in an elephant's trunk!" he cried out in surprise.

Luckily, instead of drinking the water, the elephant squirted it back out into the air. Drizzle went flying. "This is so much fun!" he squealed with delight as he landed back in the river with a big splash!

Meanwhile, the raging torrent that had forced Dribble along the river, calmed into a gentle ripple. Dribble warmed up and changed back into a droplet. As he slowly floated down the river feeling happy and relaxed, he thought, "I have time to read a book before I win the race."

However, as he turned to the first page, he unexpectedly bumped into something hard and scaly. "What is it?" he asked himself feeling a little uneasy.

As he looked up, to his horror, he saw that he was face to face with a crocodile! "Ahhhh!" he screamed in panic.

The crocodile opened his mouth, revealing his big, sharp teeth. With an almighty leap, Dribble jumped off the crocodile and plunged head first into the river. "Phew," he thought with relief. "That was a narrow escape!"

In the meadow, happily sparkling in the sun, Dazzle forgot she was in a race. Fortunately for her, a gust of wind circled the petal she was sitting on and blew it up into the sky. Up she went, soaring through the air, riding the petal like a surfboard skimming the ocean waves.

The petal landed on top of a waterfall. "Wheeeee!" Dazzle screamed as she surfed down the vertical rock of gushing water. The sun was shining and, in her excitement, she created a beautiful rainbow. A red, orange, yellow, green, blue, indigo and violet arch shimmered in the spray of the water.

Remembering the race, Dazzle jumped off the petal and dived into the river below. Back on track, she swam on determinedly.

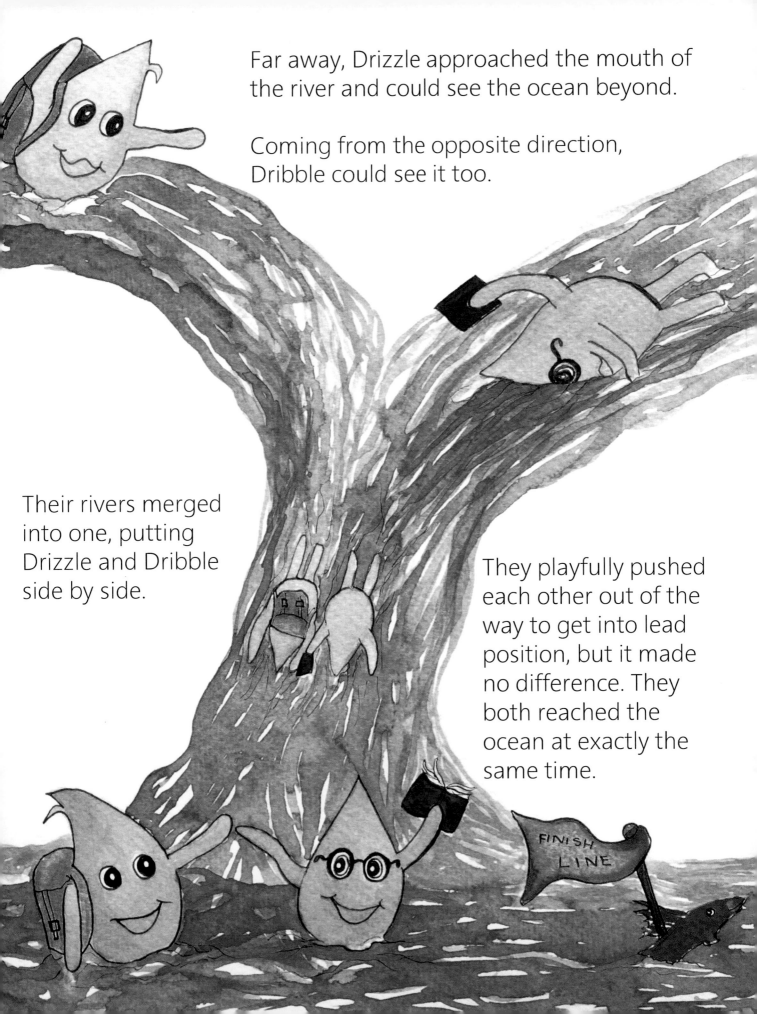

Far away, Drizzle approached the mouth of the river and could see the ocean beyond.

Coming from the opposite direction, Dribble could see it too.

Their rivers merged into one, putting Drizzle and Dribble side by side.

They playfully pushed each other out of the way to get into lead position, but it made no difference. They both reached the ocean at exactly the same time.

FINISH LINE

Although they were disappointed it was a draw, they looked at each other and laughed. Happy to see one another again, they shook hands and swapped stories about their adventures.

"Where's Dazzle?" they asked looking around, but Dazzle was nowhere to be seen.

As they swam further into the ocean trying to find her, it started to get dark. Drizzle and Dribble searched all through the night until, just before sunrise, they heard the faint sound of a beautiful song. "Where is it coming from?" asked Drizzle. In the distance, they could see mysterious, shadowy shapes slowly moving towards them.

"It's a pod of humpback whales!" exclaimed Dribble. One of the whales jumped out of the water and sprayed a misty rainbow from its blowhole. "It's Dazzle!" they cheered.

Drizzle and Dribble were very happy to see her. "Hurray! Dazzle, you are the winner of the race! You beat us to the ocean."

Dazzle was jubilant. She twirled and dived back into the water pleased to be with her teammates again.

In honour of Dazzle winning the race, the humpback whales sprayed rainbows from their blowholes all at the same time. It was like a spectacular firework display.

When the celebrations came to an end, the Daring Droplets waved goodbye to the humpback whales. "Well done to us!" declared Dribble. "We successfully completed another water cycle and now all the people, plants and animals in the world have water to drink. We make a great team."

They were very pleased and proud of themselves.

"What are we going to do now?" asked Drizzle.

"Well," replied Dazzle with a big sparkly smile, "we start all over again, of course!"

WATER CYCLE MAP

Clouds

Precipitation

Snow and ice

Run off

Ground wa...

Ocean